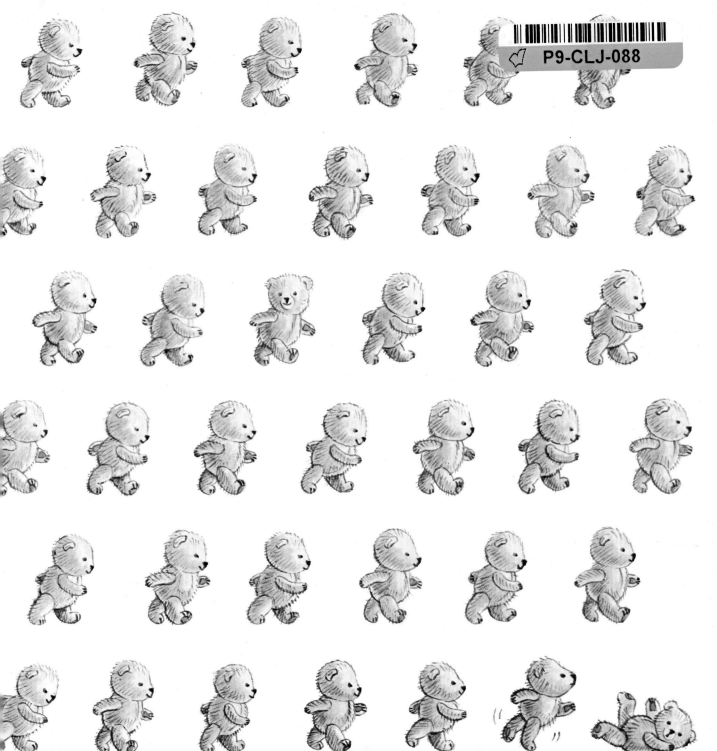

P9-CLJ-088

Teddy's
First Christmas

AMANDA DAVIDSON

Holt, Rinehart and Winston / New York

For Andrew

Text and illustrations copyright © 1982 by Amanda Davidson
All rights reserved, including the right to reproduce this
book or portions thereof in any form.
Published in the United States by Holt, Rinehart and Winston,
383 Madison Avenue, New York, New York 10017.

Library of Congress Catalog Card Number: 82-82092
ISBN: 0-03-062616-1

First American Edition
Printed in Italy
3   5   7   9   8   6   4   2

ISBN 0-03-062616-1

It is Christmas Eve. Everyone is asleep.

Look at the presents piled under the tree.

Look at the big red box with the ribbon on top.

There's somebody inside. . . .

It's Teddy!

Hello, Teddy.

"What's that?" says Teddy.

"It's very hard to reach."

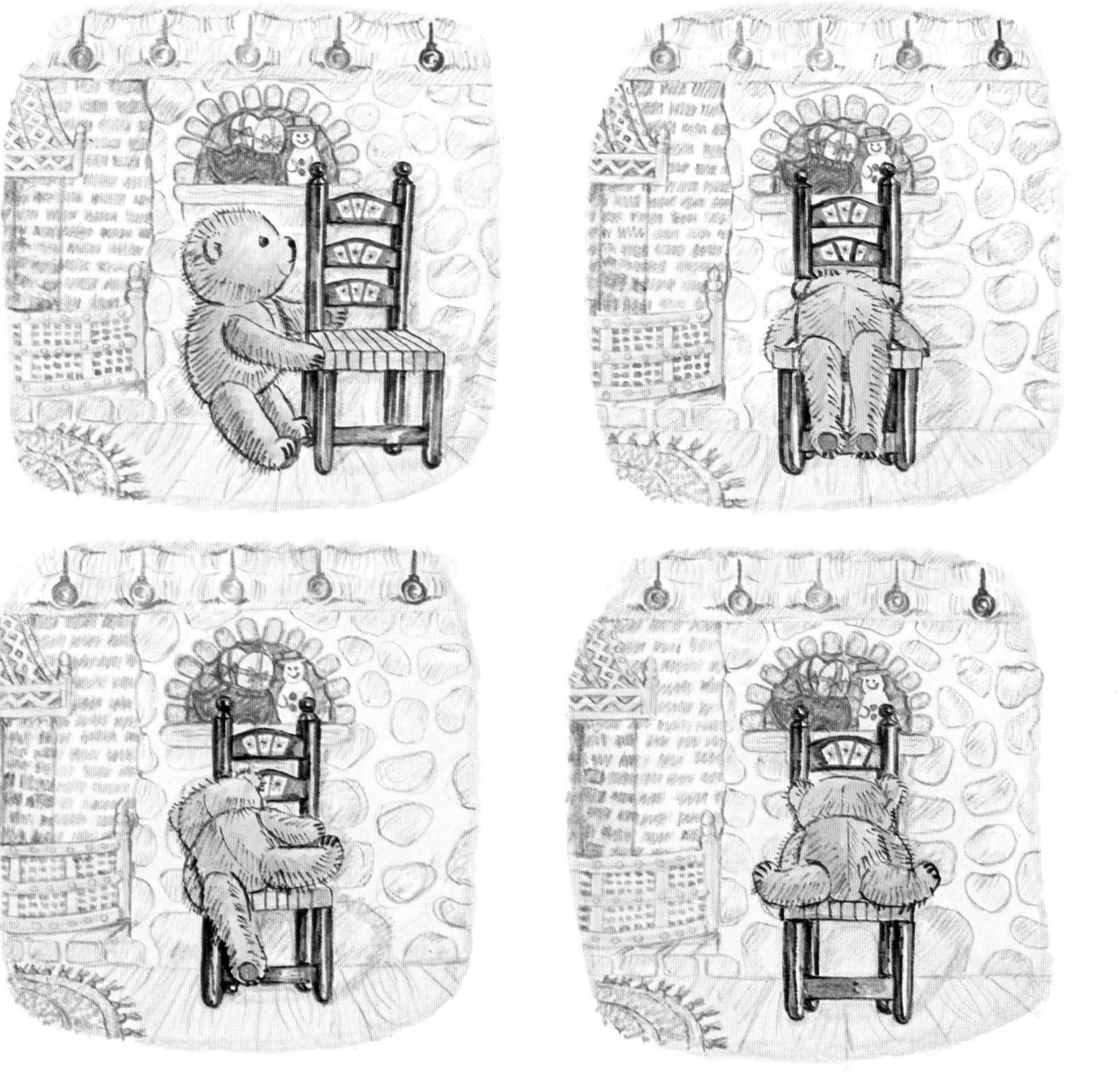

“What shall I do?”

Be *careful*, Teddy.

Oh dear! Get up, Teddy.

"Who's that?" says Teddy.

"I'd like to talk to her."

Be *careful*, Teddy.

Oh dear! There you go again.

"And what's this?" says Teddy.

"I'll pull it and see."

Pull, pull, and . . .

whoops . . .

back in the box,

ready for Christmas morning!